DRAGONBORN
Duel of Dragons

BY MICHAEL DAHL
ILLUSTRATED BY LUIGI AIME

RAINTREE IS AN IMPRINT OF CAPSTONE GLOBAL LIBRARY LIMITED, A COMPANY INCORPORATED IN
ENGLAND AND WALES HAVING ITS REGISTERED OFFICE AT 264 BANBURY ROAD, OXFORD, OX2 7DY -
REGISTERED COMPANY NUMBER: 6695582

WWW.RAINTREE.CO.UK
MYORDERS@RAINTREE.CO.UK

TEXT © CAPSTONE GLOBAL LIBRARY LIMITED 2019
THE MORAL RIGHTS OF THE PROPRIETOR HAVE BEEN ASSERTED.

ART DIRECTOR: KAY FRASER
GRAPHIC DESIGNER: HILARY WACHOLZ
PRODUCTION SPECIALIST: KATHY MCCOLLEY
ORIGINAL ILLUSTRATIONS © 2013
ILLUSTRATED BY LUIGI AIME
ORIGINATED BY CAPSTONE GLOBAL LIBRARY LTD
Printed and bound in the United Kingdom.

ISBN 978 1 4747 7147 4
22 21 20 19 18
10 9 8 7 6 5 4 3 2 1

BRITISH LIBRARY CATALOGUING IN PUBLICATION DATA
A FULL CATALOGUE RECORD FOR THIS BOOK IS AVAILABLE FROM THE BRITISH LIBRARY.

ACKNOWLEDGEMENTS
SHUTTERSTOCK: CAESART (METAL PLATE, PP. 1, 4, 66); FERNANDO CORTES (DRAGON PATTERN)

EVERY EFFORT HAS BEEN MADE TO CONTACT COPYRIGHT HOLDERS OF MATERIAL REPRODUCED IN THIS
BOOK. ANY OMISSIONS WILL BE RECTIFIED IN SUBSEQUENT PRINTINGS IF NOTICE IS GIVEN TO THE
PUBLISHER.

CONTENTS

A NEW AGE OF DRAGONS HAS BEGUN.

DRAGONBORN

Young people around the world
have discovered that dragon blood
flows in their veins. They are filled
with new power and new ideas.
But before they reveal themselves
to the world, they must find one
another . . .

CHAPTER 1
Empty chains

A stone tower stood in the middle of a lonely forest.

Leaves crunched underfoot and twigs snapped.

A teenage boy walked through the thick maze of trees. His name was Sam Stevens.

When he saw the stone tower, Sam
stopped.

He stared at the tower's open door
and frowned.

"It's been a long time," he said to
himself.

Inside the tower was a single, large room.

Dust and dead leaves covered the floor. Darkness lurked in the corners.

Chains hung from the far wall.

As Sam stepped into the room, a cool wind stirred the chains.

They scraped against the stone wall. He remembered that scraping sound.

He could not forget the time he had lived within the tower.

His parents had been ashamed of him.

They had been afraid of him.

They had kept him chained inside the tower every afternoon as soon as he came home from school.

They said it was for his own good.

That was six schools ago.

Sam rubbed his arm. On his skin was a birthmark in the shape of a dragon.

He didn't have to see it to know that the mark was glowing.

He could feel it through the sleeve of his jacket.

It happened whenever the dragon part of him started growing stronger.

The wind stirred the chains again.

Sam sniffed the air. Someone was nearby.

The tower room was empty, so he turned towards the door.

Outside, the woods were growing darker.

Beyond the treetops, the sky was dark blue.

Sam sniffed the air again. A strange odour stung his nose.

It smelled wild, but familiar.

Then he saw three shadows moving among the trees.

CHAPTER 2
Strangers

Sam grabbed his arm.

His birthmark felt like fire.

Three strangers walked through the door. Two boys and a girl.

The boys looked the same age as Sam.

One of the boys wore a hood pulled over his head. He stepped forward and asked, "Are you Sam Stevens?"

Sam rubbed his arm again. "Who are you?" he asked the strangers.

The girl had long red hair. She tilted her head and her hair swept across her face. It covered one of her eyes. "Are you Sam Stevens?" she asked.

"What if I am?" said Sam.

The hooded boy smiled. "Don't be ashamed of who you are," he said. "It's a simple question."

"What are you talking about?" Sam asked angrily.

The hooded boy pointed at the chains on the wall. "My parents did that to me too," he said.

"I don't know what you're talking about," said Sam.

"Don't you?" asked the hooded boy. He lifted his head, and Sam could see his eyes beneath his hood.

They were orange, like clouds in a sunset.

Sam closed his eyes. He remembered when he had been chained up in that tower.

Some nights, a mighty wind would shake the trees outside. A dark shape would roar in the darkness.

Sam had tried hard to see what it was. He could only see a shadow.

The shadow had wings and gleaming orange eyes.

Sam opened his eyes and stared at the boy.

"That was you?" Sam asked.

The boy nodded. "I'm Jager," he said. "I had escaped. And I was looking for someone like me."

The second boy, with shaggy blonde hair, nodded. "We all were," he said.

He lifted up his sleeve.

So did Jager and the red-haired girl.

They each had a birthmark shaped like a dragon.

CHAPTER 3
A challenge

"Why did you come here?" Sam asked.

"Why did *you* come?" asked Jager.

Sam looked at the empty chains hanging from the wall. "I wanted to see this place," he said. "One last time."

Sam put his hands in his jacket pockets. "I'm moving away from here," he said.

Sam stared at the three strangers. "You never answered my question," he said. "Why are you here?"

"We're here for you, of course," said the blonde boy. "We need a leader."

The red-haired girl laughed.

Jager frowned and made a noise – a growl.

"Is this a joke?" asked Sam.

"No joke," said Jager. "We need to stick together. With our own kind. And we need a leader."

"I'm no leader," said Sam.

"I agree," said Jager. "But we have to find out for ourselves."

Sam wanted to ask him another question, but a breeze rushed through the room. The breeze was strong, and it was loud.

Jager raised his face and his hood slipped off his head. His orange eyes blazed in the dim light.

He threw off his sweatshirt, and two wide wings grew from his shoulders.

Then he roared.

It was a roar familiar to Sam.

The dragon that was Jager rose into the air.

The creature beat its wings. It tore through the roof of the tower and disappeared into the dark woods.

"Where did he go?" asked Sam.

"He's waiting for you," said the girl.

"For the challenge," added the blonde boy.

"You have to battle with him to determine who will be the leader," said the girl.

"What? Why me?" asked Sam.

"Because he's already defeated us," said the boy.

"It's what dragons do," said the girl.

It was the craziest thing Sam had ever heard. But the girl's words seemed to calm him. His birthmark was no longer burning.

He smelled the wild odour again. It seemed to call him out into the darkness.

"Fighting is what animals do," said Sam. "I'm not an animal."

The blonde boy shook his head. "But you're not exactly human either, are you?" he asked.

The red-haired girl stepped forward. "Don't be ashamed of who you are," she said.

That's what Jager said, Sam thought.

He looked up through the damaged roof.

Stars shone in the sky. Their burning light seemed to pull at him.

Sam looked down at his feet. He was floating above the floor.

CHAPTER 4
Wing to wing

Two wings had unfolded from Sam's back. He hadn't been able to stop them ripping through his top and stretching from wall to wall.

"You can't help it, can you," said the blonde boy. "It's who you are."

"Who we all are," said the girl.

A roar ripped through the sky. *He's waiting for me*, thought Sam.

Sam was fully a dragon. He rose through the roof with ease.

The night air felt cool against his scales. His tail whipped back and forth.

He gazed down and saw the boy and girl looking up at him.

They were changing before his eyes.

In a moment, the tower room was filled with wings and claws and blazing eyes.

Then they rose up to meet him. Sam heard another roar.

A blue-black cloud glistened in the moonlight. No, it wasn't a cloud.

It was Jager, his wings outspread and his jaws open wide.

Meet me! cried Jager.

Sam was surprised.

He understood the other dragon's words.

But it was a sound inside his head rather than in his dragon ears.

The blue dragon reared up and bellowed.

Without thinking, Sam bellowed back. *I'm here*, he replied.

He was answering Jager's challenge, dragon to dragon.

Yes, he thought. *This is what I have to do.* It was who he was.

Sam did not feel any fear. Instead, he felt a rush of power.

He spread his wings, matching Jager.

For a second, the two dragons faced each other without moving.

They hung like huge bats in the sky.

Then they charged.

Jager rushed towards Sam. The flapping of his huge wings sounded like thunder.

Swiftly, Jager's massive, horned
head struck the centre of Sam's chest.
Sam bellowed and fell back.

Tumbling backwards, Sam
panicked. He wasn't used to flying,
or to falling.

The dragons were fighting high
above the forest.

Sam lashed his tail. It felt like a
third arm to him.

He used it to balance his new, unfamiliar weight.

Sam's wings beat against the air, helping to turn him around.

His clawed feet brushed against the treetops. He steadied himself in the darkness.

Jager was not far away.

Suddenly, the two young dragons rushed at each other again. This time they each swiped at each other with their leathery wings.

Sam felt the blow, but Jager staggered too. *Ha!* thought Sam. *Maybe I'm getting the hang of this.*

From the corner of one of his lizard eyes, Sam saw the other two dragons. They were hanging back.

They flapped their wings smoothly and slowly.

They were watching patiently, waiting for the battle to be over.

You can do it!

Sam thought he heard a voice inside his head. Maybe it was from the blonde boy dragon.

Again and again, Jager was the first to attack. He would swoop down on Sam and bite at his wing, his neck, his torso. Then he would fly away.

It was as if he was teasing Sam. *Give me a real fight!*

Sam was still getting used to his new body. He struck back, just not as expertly as Jager.

But Sam learned quickly. He copied Jager and swooped and soared and somersaulted.

The fight seemed to last for hours. *Does time flow differently for dragons?* Sam wondered.

Back and forth, he and Jager struck at each other. First one, then the other, seemed to be the winner.

The moon was setting beneath the trees and neither of them was ready to surrender.

Sam was surprised by the energy in his dragon body. His new muscles seemed to move and work on their own. His scales no longer felt heavy. They felt comforting, protecting.

He flapped his wings and hovered in place.

He gazed at Jager, wondering where and how to strike next.

Suddenly, Jager roared and soared straight up. Sam quickly followed.

Cold, wet air brushed against his wings. The two of them were passing through a layer of clouds.

The thick mist blinded Sam. He was swallowed up in thick darkness.

Then Sam saw a pair of dark, green wings diving towards him.

A pair of jaws opened.

A stream of flame shot from the creature's throat.

It wasn't Jager.

It was another dragon.

CHAPTER 5
Ambush

The green dragon's flames hurtled towards Sam.

Sam was too shocked to think clearly. Who was this creature?

The fire singed the edge of Sam's right wing. He bellowed in pain.

If Sam had been in his human shape, the fire would have killed him. His dragon scales saved him. They shielded him from the worst of the flames.

Still, the pain was terrible.

Jager! cried Sam with his dragon tongue. He quickly flew through the clouds. He fled towards the forest, hidden somewhere below him.

The new dragon was close behind.

Fire shot from the stranger's mouth again.

This time Sam swerved and dipped. The fire streamed past his head.

Where is Jager? Sam wondered. *And where are the other two?*

Sam burst out of the clouds. He saw a familiar shape below him.

The tower.

CHAPTER 6
Plan of attack

Dark figures hovered around the edge of the tower.

He heard a voice. *Down here*, the red-haired girl-dragon called. *Into the tower*.

Sam looked down and smiled. The green dragon was still close behind him.

Sam plunged down, falling fast towards the tower. Streams of fire shot all around him as he fell.

Sam suddenly folded his wings, slowing his speed. He extended his scaled feet towards the tower's floor. It seemed to rise up to meet him.

His deadly attacker was still in pursuit.

Sam landed on the cold stone floor.

Just as the green dragon reached the edge of the broken roof, flames shot out from three sides at it.

The three dragons had planned a surprise attack.

The green dragon screamed and shrieked in pain. It spun in a whirl of scales and talons and flashing fangs.

Its heavy emerald wings beat angrily against the fiery air.

Then, with a final cry, it flew up from the roof and vanished into the clouds.

Sam stared up at the sky. With a human hand, he rubbed the back of his aching neck.

The three other dragons quietly landed beside him. A wind blew through the room. Then they, too, were human.

"Who was that?" asked Sam. He was shaking.

"Someone like us," said Jager. "He just wanted to spoil our fun."

Sam felt an unexpected surge of pride.

Who would have thought, when he came back to this horrible place, that he would have ended up fighting a creature of such power?

"But we still don't have a leader," said the blonde boy.

"That's right," agreed the girl. "Your battle never really ended."

Sam stuck his hand out and shook Jager's. "No leader yet," said Sam. "But we do have a team."

AUTHOR

Michael Dahl is the author of more than 200 books for children and young adults. He has won the AEP Distinguished Achievement Award three times for his non-fiction. His Finnegan Zwake mystery series was shortlisted twice by the Anthony and Agatha awards. He has also written the Dragonblood series. He is a featured speaker at conferences around the United States on graphic novels and high-interest books for boys.

ILLUSTRATOR

Luigi Aime was born in 1987 in Savigliano, a small Italian city near Turin. Even at the age of three, he loved to draw. He attended art school, graduating with honours in Illustration and Animation from the European Institute of Design in Milan, Italy.

DISCUSSION QUESTIONS

1. Why did Sam return to the tower?

2. Why are the people with dragon blood trying to find each other?

3. What questions do you still have about this story? Discuss them!

WRITING PROMPTS

1. What happens after this book ends? Write a short story that extends the story.

2. It can be very interesting to think about a story from another person's point of view. Try writing this story, or part of it, from Jager's point of view. What does he see, hear, think and say? What does he notice? How is the story different?

3. Create a cover for a book. It can be this book or another book you like, or a made-up book. Write the information on the back, and include the author and illustrator names.

GLOSSARY

ashamed embarrassed

attention concentration or notice

bellowed shouted or roared

birthmark mark on the skin that has been there since birth

challenge test or trial

determine decide

familiar well-known or easily recognized

odour smell

singed burned

surge sudden, strong increase

unexpected surprising

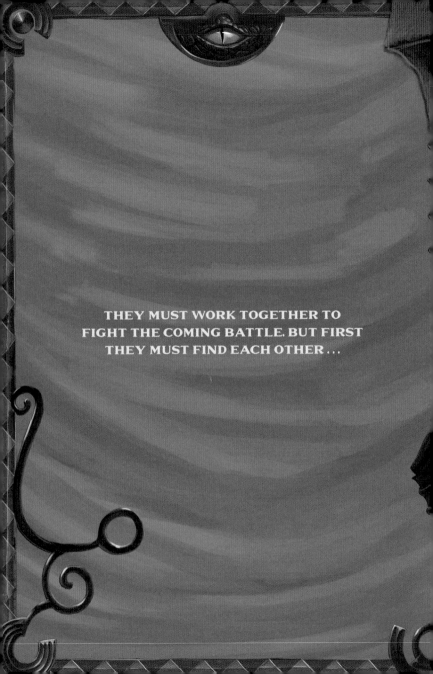

THEY MUST WORK TOGETHER TO
FIGHT THE COMING BATTLE. BUT FIRST
THEY MUST FIND EACH OTHER ...

SAM STEVENS

When Sam was five years old, a strange dog came through the woods. It stared at him and growled. Sam's hands changed to claws and he growled back! The dog ran away. That's when Sam – and his mother – realized that he was different.

Age: 16
Hometown: Outside Olympia, Washington, USA
Dragon appearance: Deep orange
Dragon species: *Draconis fortis* ("fearless dragon")
Strength: Leadership

DRAGONBLOOD
RUNS THROUGH THEIR VEINS...